OOEY GOOEY SURPRISE

For my twin who shares the memories. And for my son, a tinkerer like our pop. K.M.

For the very messy bakers in my house. L.A.

OOEY GOOEY SURPRISE

Story by Karen Mowbray
Illustrations by Lisa Allen

BATEMAN BOOKS

HAPPY BIRTHDAY
POP

A birthday banner stuck to a tree,
party plates out for afternoon tea.
Balloons blown up, streamers strung,
ready for Pop to arrive at one.

Dad was mowing the overgrown lawn,
singing away with headphones on.
Mum hollered out, 'Be good, Joe, please!
I'm off to get Pop,' she said, waving her keys.

'Down the drive, out the gate,
out of sight, no time to wait!'

A wave to Dad and off I sprint
to find Mum's trusty baking tin!
With a grand idea and speedy feet,
I race to bake my pop a treat.

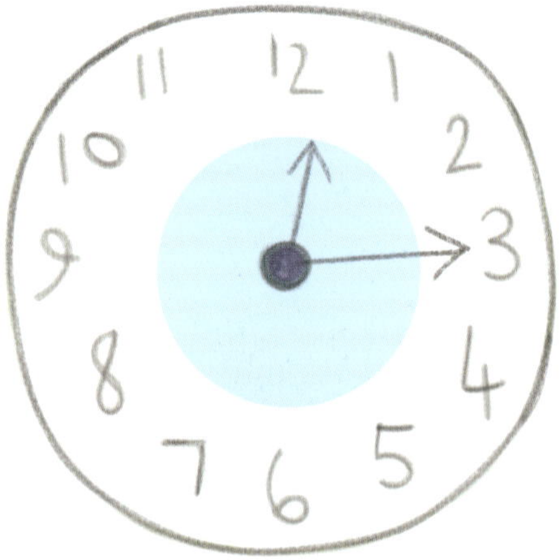

Into the kitchen, fridge open wide,
I look for ingredients inside.

Milk and butter; we have plenty.
Eggs — oh no! — the container's empty.

Sauce
BUTTER
Cream
JUICE
JAM

Past the toolshed, running fast,
a quick swing under the monkey bars.

Into the coop, down I bend,
keeping an eye out for Mrs Hen.
That vicious chook is not so nice.
She's tried to peck me once or twice!

Kneeling down, staying calm,
searching her box
with an outstretched arm ...

Got one!
Quickly, out I go.

Stumble … fumble …

Whoops!
Oh no!

Ooey, gooey, slimy egg;
dripping, trickling, down my head.

I need an egg, not a mess!
I'll have to go back to the nest!

Feeling brave, in I hurry,
but Mrs Hen is in a flurry!
Flapping wings, an angry look;
she's very fierce, that mean old chook!

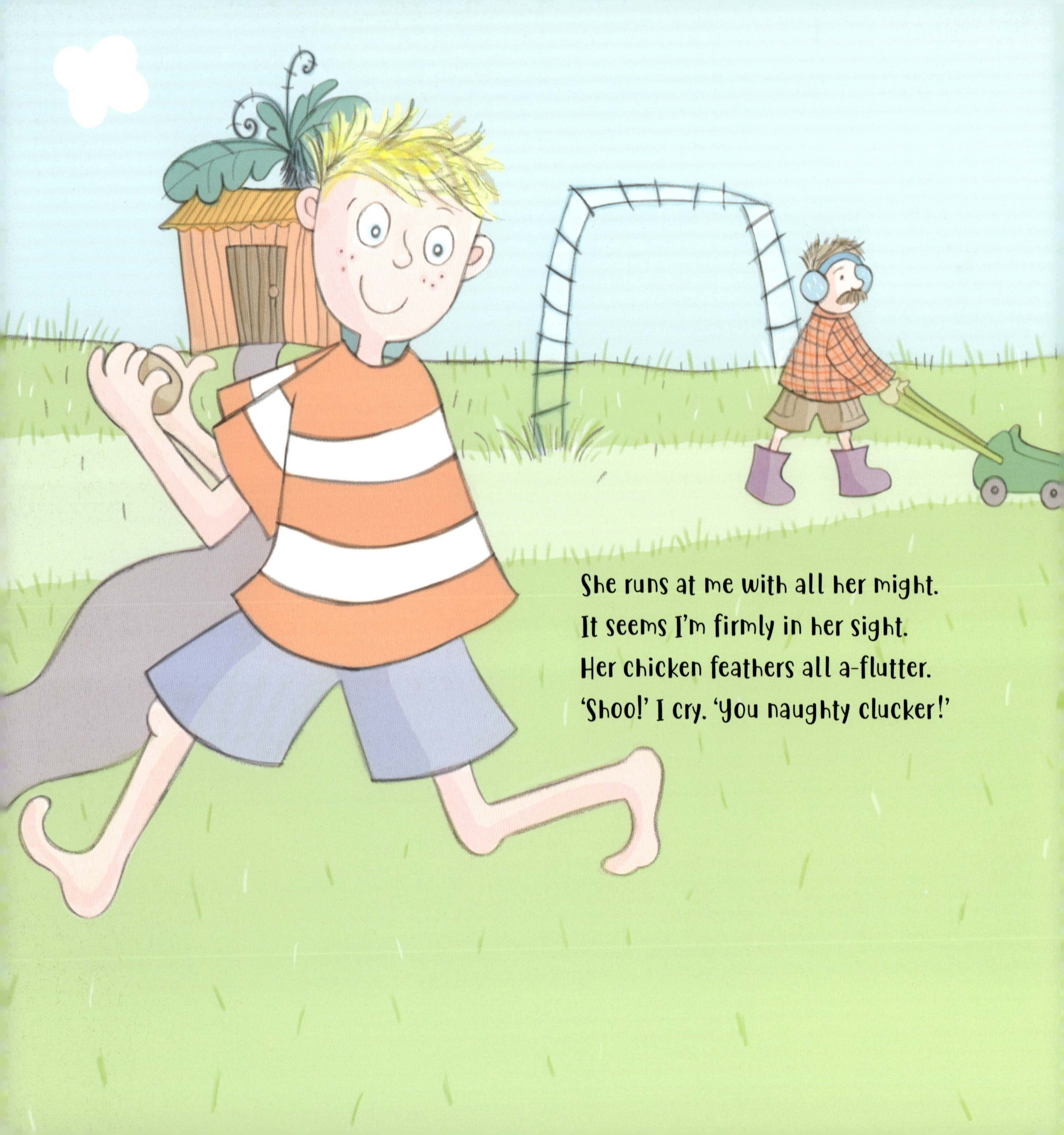

She runs at me with all her might.
It seems I'm firmly in her sight.
Her chicken feathers all a-flutter.
'Shoo!' I cry. 'You naughty clucker!'

Grabbing an egg, I sprint out fast.
I dash back under the monkey bars.
Escaping the chook, I run like mad,
past the toolshed, right past Dad.

Dad waves at me, I wave back.
Now into the kitchen, back on track.
That was close! Must press on.
Mum will be back before too long.

I get the milk, the flour, a bowl;
the mixer, a spoon — under control!
Up on a stool, stretching tall,
tippy-toe balancing; I won't fall!

Adding ingredients
to make my cake,
milk is heavy,
I start to shake!

Bottle is tipping.
Bowl is filling.
Some going in.
Some of it spilling!

I try to get the milk to pour ...

Struggling ... juggling ...

Oops ... on floor!

Ooey, gooey, slippery splatter!
Mum says accidents don't matter.
Oopsie daise, this isn't great.
Milky mess will have to wait.

Still some mixture left to bake
so I can finish Pop's birthday cake.
Need to hurry. Not much time.
I set the cake mixer to high.

The mixer churns. It mixes well.
My cake is looking super swell.
Mixer starts to mix things faster.
It seems I AM a baking master!

Mixer humming, seems alright,
buzzing noise gives me a fright.

What is happening? The mixer's shaking.
Something's wrong with what I'm making!

Churning, groaning, it jumps and bumps,
spitting out mixture in puddles and clumps!

Mixer's mixing faster, faster!

Splattering ... scattering ...

A DISASTER!

SUPERMIX

Mixer comes to a sudden halt.
Kitchen's a mess. It's all my fault!
Mum is going to be so mad.
Keep calm, I think.
I could blame Dad?

Just then the car pulls up the drive.
Mum and Pop are just outside!
Out they get, I see them coming;
I hear the mower no longer running!

They're almost here . . . 'Argh!' I cry.
I close the door to the mess and sigh.
Mum sees me covered in egg and cake.
'OH, JOE!' she growls. 'For Goodness' sake!'

Hands on hips, Mum raises her brow.
I smile and try to look sweet somehow.
Pop is smirking, so is Dad.
'I was making a cake. Don't be mad.
A scrummy, yummy birthday treat
that now Pop cannot even eat.'

‘Mum, maybe you should close your eyes …’

'Happy Birthday, Pop...

SURPRISE!'

David Bateman Ltd,
Unit 2/5 Workspace Drive, Hobsonville, Auckland 0618, New Zealand
www.batemanbooks.co.nz

A catalogue record for this book is available from the National Library of New Zealand.

ISBN: 978-1-77689-013-2

Karen Mowbray is a primary school teacher. She has taught children of all ages in the private and state sectors both in New Zealand and overseas. Karen has been writing for children for several years. She lives with her husband and three children in Matangi, New Zealand. This is her second picture book.

Lisa Allen is an illustrator and designer based in Muriwai, on Auckland's west coast. She has illustrated a number of picture books in a variety of different styles.

Design by Lisa Allen
Printed in China by Toppan Leefung Printing Ltd